A NOTE TO PARENTS

When your children are ready to "step into reading," giving them the right books—and lots of them—is as crucial as giving them the right food to eat. **Step into Reading Books** present exciting stories and information reinforced with lively, colorful illustrations that make learning to read fun, satisfying, and worthwhile. They are priced so that acquiring an entire library of them is affordable. And they are beginning readers with an important difference—they're written on four levels.

Step 1 Books, with their very large type and extremely simple vocabulary, have been created for the very youngest readers. **Step 2 Books** are both longer and slightly more difficult. **Step 3 Books,** written to mid-second-grade reading levels, are for the child who has acquired even greater reading skills. **Step 4 Books** offer exciting nonfiction for the increasingly proficient reader.

Children develop at different ages. **Step into Reading Books,** with their four levels of reading, are designed to help children become good—and interested—readers *faster*. The grade levels assigned to the four steps—preschool through grade 1 for Step 1, grades 1 through 3 for Step 2, grades 2 and 3 for Step 3, and grades 2 through 4 for Step 4—are intended only as guides. Some children move through all four steps very rapidly; others climb the steps over a period of several years. These books will help your child "step into reading" in style!

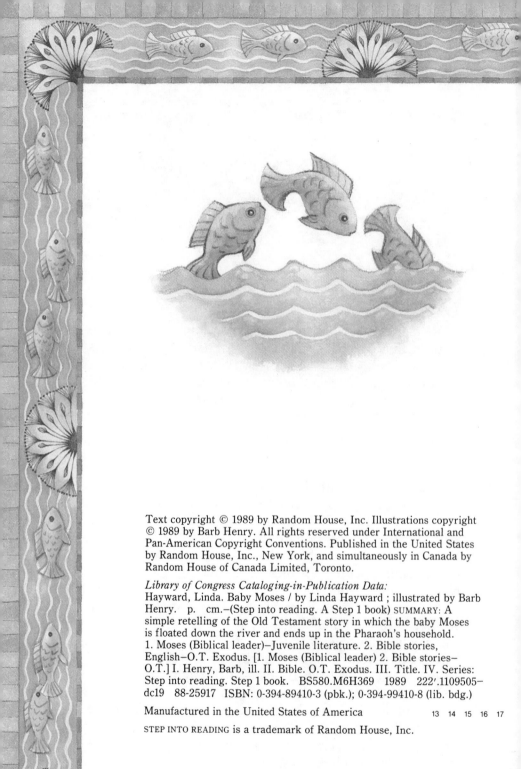

Library of Congress Cataloging-in-Publication Data:
Hayward, Linda. Baby Moses / by Linda Hayward ; illustrated by Barb Henry.   p.   cm.–(Step into reading. A Step 1 book) SUMMARY: A simple retelling of the Old Testament story in which the baby Moses is floated down the river and ends up in the Pharaoh's household. 1. Moses (Biblical leader)–Juvenile literature. 2. Bible stories, English–O.T. Exodus. [1. Moses (Biblical leader) 2. Bible stories– O.T.] I. Henry, Barb, ill. II. Bible. O.T. Exodus. III. Title. IV. Series: Step into reading. Step 1 book.   BS580.M6H369   1989   222′.1109505– dc19   88-25917   ISBN: 0-394-89410-3 (pbk.); 0-394-99410-8 (lib. bdg.)

Manufactured in the United States of America   13 14 15 16 17

STEP INTO READING is a trademark of Random House, Inc.

Step into Reading

Baby Moses

By Linda Hayward
Illustrated by Barb Henry

A Step 1 Book

Random House New York

Long ago
in the land
of Egypt
a baby boy
was born.

His mother
had to save
him from
the wicked
Pharaoh.

So she went down
to the Nile River
and made a basket
out of bulrushes.

She put the baby
in the basket.
She put the basket
in the river.

Pharaoh would not
find him there!

Was the baby safe?

"Not yet!"
said the snakes
that wiggled
in the sand.

"Not yet!"
said the birds
that waded
near the bank.

"Not yet!"
said the hippos
that sank down
in the water.

"Not yet!"
said the crocodiles
that floated
on top.

The basket floated
down the Nile
and right past
Pharaoh's garden.

Pharaoh's daughter
saw the basket.

What was inside?

Oh, a baby!

She wanted
to take care
of him.

Pharaoh found out.
He said the baby
must die.

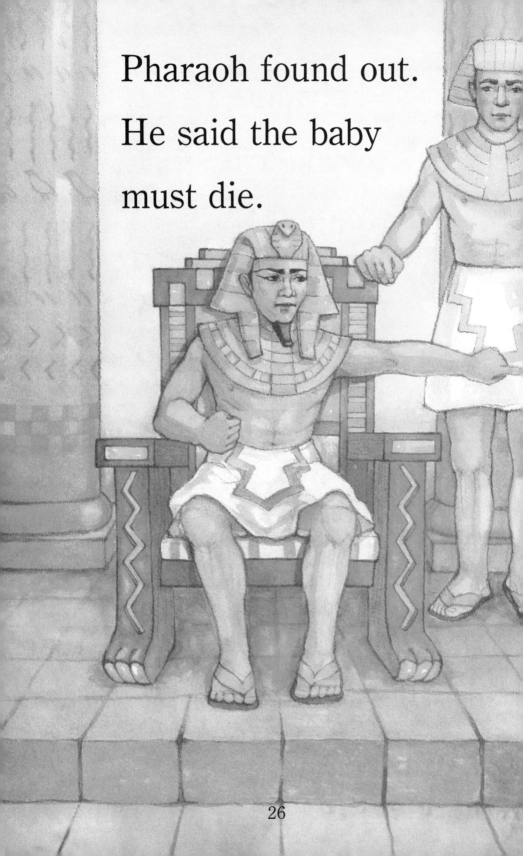

"I call him Moses,"
said the princess.

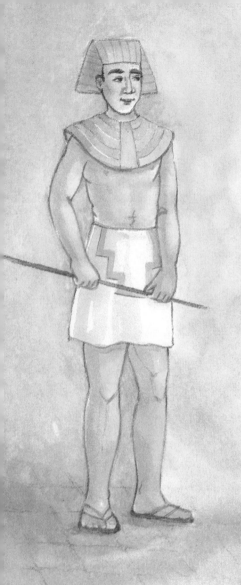

Pharaoh let her keep the baby because he loved his daughter.

Then was the baby safe?

Yes!

Baby Moses was as safe

as a prince

in Pharaoh's house.

And
when Moses
grew up,
he saved his
people from
the wicked
Pharaoh.